MARGRET & H. A. REY'

Sweet Dreams, Curious George

Written by Cynthia Platt

illustrated in the style of H. A. Rey *by* Mary O'Keefe Young

HOUGHTON MIFFLIN HARCOURT
Boston   New York

To Barbara and Doc, with love — C.P.
For my sweet dreamers — Bridget, Matt, Tara, and Autumn — M.O'K.Y.

Permissions
Houghton Mifflin Harcourt Publishing Company
215 Park Avenue South
New York, New York 10003

www.hmhco.com

The text of this book is Adobe Garamond.

ISBN 978-0-544-03880-6 hardcover
ISBN 978-0-544-50321-2 paperback

Manufactured in China
SCP 10 9 8 7 6 5 4 3 2 1

4500557827

This is George. George is a good little monkey and always very curious.

Today, he's curious about a library book that his friend the man with the yellow hat brought home.

George sat down to look at the book. There was a yellow chick on the cover, pointing up to the sky. This made George even more curious.

He brought it to the
man with the yellow hat.

"Why don't we wait until after dinner, George?" asked his friend.
"Then we can read it as a bedtime story."

George wanted to read the book . . . but he was feeling hungry
and dinner did smell delicious.

After dinner, it was bathtime. A nice warm bath is just what a monkey needs after a long day! George played with his rubber ducky and little toy boat until it was time to get out.

His friend held out a fluffy towel with a hood that looked like a chick.

That made George think of his new library book!

George put on his pajamas and hopped into bed. He couldn't wait to hear that story!

"This is the story of Chicken Little," said the man with the yellow hat. "I think you're going to like this one, George!"

George did like it! Poor Chicken Little thought the sky was going to fall, and then lots of other animals thought it would too. Thank goodness, the sky didn't actually fall. Little monkeys like happy endings.

It seemed like the perfect bedtime story . . .

One day Chicke
Little was scratch
for food when an
acorn fell from a
tree and hit her head

That is, until George woke up in the middle of the night! He had
had a terrible dream that the sky really was falling.
George was scared.

His friend came to see what was the matter. George pointed to the book and then to the ceiling.

"Don't worry, George—it was just a dream," said his friend. "The sky isn't really going to fall. Let's try to relax and get back to sleep."

First, the man with the yellow hat brought him a cup of warm milk. "Warm milk always makes me feel sleepy, George."

It seemed to be working for George, too, until—oh, no!—the warm milk spilled all over the place.

After cleaning the mess, his friend got another book to read.

The story was about a train that had to race along the tracks to deliver a special package to a little girl. It was very exciting.

George was even more wide awake than before!

"Maybe a song will help," said the man with the yellow hat. "Lie down in bed and I'll sing to you."

George tried to rest. He really did. But the song was pretty catchy. First he tapped his toes slowly. Then his whole body wanted to dance!

He got up and bounced on the bed.

"Hmm," said his friend. "I wish I knew why you can't sleep tonight!"

George stopped dancing. He pulled out the book *Chicken Little* and then pointed to the ceiling again, frowning.

"Are you still worried that the sky is going to fall?" his friend asked.
George nodded. He just couldn't get that dream out of his head.

"Hmm . . ." said his friend. "I have an idea. Why don't we
take my telescope outside to look at the stars and make sure
the sky is still way up where it should be?"

George liked that idea so much that he leaped right out of
his bed.

It was chilly outside, but it was very nice to be out in the dark of the night, too. The stars were still up in the sky, far, far away.

The man with the yellow hat set up the telescope and showed George how to look through it.

When George looked through the telescope, the stars looked quite near. He could even see planets!

Near . . . far . . . near . . . far. He looked through the telescope many times. It was like magic.

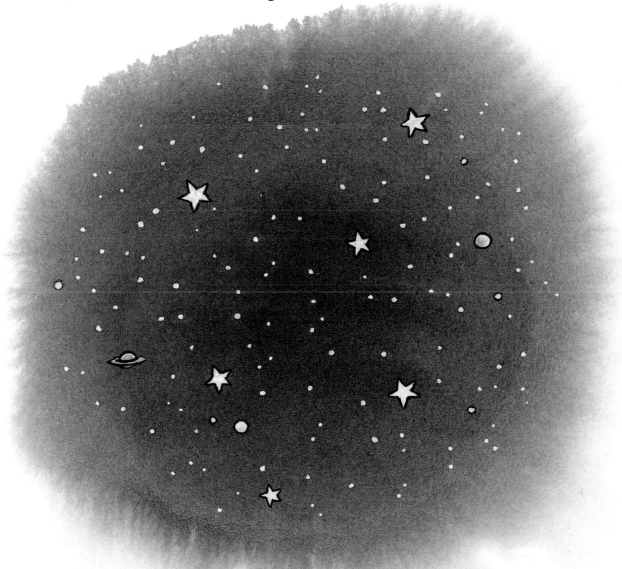

"See, George?" asked his friend. "The stars are just where they should be. That sky doesn't look like it's falling, does it?"

George shook his head with a smile.

The man with the yellow hat even had a chart with something called constellations on them—pictures in the stars!

George loved looking for the constellations so much that he completely forgot about his bad dream.

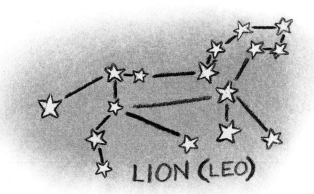

LION (LEO)

But it was so late! George yawned.

"I think it's time for both of us to get to sleep, George," said his friend, leading him back into the house.

By the time they got back to George's room, he was very tired.

His friend gave him a hug and tucked him in tightly.

"Good night, George," said the man with the yellow hat as he was about to close the door. "I hope you have happy dreams."

George cuddled his teddy bear for a minute, and then started to fret again, just a teeny bit, about the sky falling.

He hopped out of bed and opened his curtains so that he could see the stars and the sky, right where they should be.

As the starlight streamed into his bedroom, George
snuggled down deep into his blankets and fell asleep.

Sweet dreams, George!